A Letter to a Young Poet

by

Virginia Woolf

Written in 1932.

British Library Cataloguing-in-Publication Data
A catalogue record for this book is available from the
British Library

Virginia Woolf

Virginia Woolf was born Adeline Virginia Stephen in Kensington, London, England in 1882. Her father, Leslie Stephen, was a respected man of letters, and as a young girl Woolf was introduced to many literary figures, including Henry James. Woolf also made great use of the family home's vast library, working her way through much of the English literary canon as a teenager. Her summers were spent in St. Ives, Cornwall, which would later form the setting for her famous novel, To the Lighthouse.

In 1895, when Woolf was just thirteen, her mother died, triggering the first of her many mental breakdowns. Despite this, between 1897 and 1901 she was able to take courses in Greek, Latin, German and history at the Ladies' Department of King's College London. She even began publishing work with the Times Literary Supplement. However, in 1904, following the death of her father, Woolf suffered another breakdown which saw her briefly institutionalised.

Following her discharge, Woolf and her sisters moved from their family home to a new abode in Bloomsbury. It was here that Woolf met Lytton Strachey, John Maynard Keynes, E. M. Forster and various other writers and intellectuals, who together would form the famous Bloomsbury Set. In 1912, Woolf married author Leonard Woolf, who nursed her through another breakdown and suicide attempt. Woolf published her first novel, The Voyage Out, in 1915. This, as well as various essays, quickly established her as a major public intellectual.

During the twenties, Woolf published the novels that established her as a leading figure of modernism and one of the greatest British novelists of the 20th century: Jacob's Room (1922), Mrs. Dalloway (1925), To the Lighthouse (1927) and Orlando (1928). Stylistically, Woolf experimented with a lyrical stream-of-consciousness narrative mode, and is now considered – along with fellow modernist James Joyce – one of the finest innovators in the English language. Her work has been translated into fifty languages, and her major novels have never been out of print.

After completing her last novel, Between the Acts, Woolf fell into a period of deep depression – exacerbated by the the onset of World War II and the destruction of her home during the Blitz. In 1941, fearing a total mental collapse, Woolf committed suicide. She was 59 years old.

A Letter to a Young Poet |

My Dear John,

Did you ever meet, or was he before your day, that old gentleman — I forget his name — who used to enliven conversation, especially at breakfast when the post came in, by saying that the art of letter-writing is dead? The penny post, the old gentleman used to say, has killed the art of letter-writing. Nobody, he continued, examining an envelope through his eye-glasses, has the time even to cross their t's. We rush, he went on, spreading his toast with marmalade, to the telephone. We commit our half-formed thoughts in ungrammatical phrases to the post card. Gray is dead, he continued; Horace Walpole is dead; Madame de Sévigné— she is dead too, I suppose he was about to add, but a fit of choking cut him short, and he had to leave the room before he had time to condemn all the arts, as his pleasure was, to the cemetery. But when the post came in this morning and I opened your letter stuffed with little blue sheets written all over in a cramped but not illegible hand — I regret to say, however, that several t's were uncrossed and the grammar of one sentence seems to me dubious — I replied after all these years to that elderly necrophilist — Nonsense. The art of letter-writing has only just come into existence. It is the child of the penny post. And there is some truth in that remark, I think. Naturally when a letter cost half a crown to send, it had to prove itself a document of some importance; it was read aloud; it was tied up with green silk; after a certain number of years it was published for the infinite delectation of posterity. But your letter, on the contrary, will have to be burnt. It only cost three-halfpence to send. Therefore you could afford to be intimate, irreticent, indiscreet in the extreme. What you tell me about poor dear C. and his adventure on the Channel boat is deadly private; your ribald jests at the expense of M. would certainly ruin your friendship if they got about; I doubt, too, that posterity, unless it is much quicker in the wit than I expect, could follow the line of your thought from the roof which leaks ("splash, splash, splash into the soap dish") past Mrs. Gape, the charwoman, whose retort to the greengrocer gives me the keenest pleasure, via Miss Curtis and her odd confidence on the steps of the omnibus; to Siamese cats ("Wrap their noses in an old stocking my Aunt says if they howl"); so to the value of criticism to a writer; so to Donne; so to Gerard Hopkins; so to tombstones; so to gold-fish; and so with a sudden alarming swoop to "Do write and tell me where poetry's going, or if it's dead?" No, your letter, because it is a true letter — one that can neither be read aloud now, nor printed in time to come — will have to be burnt. Posterity must live upon Walpole and Madame de Sévigné. The great age of letter-writing, which is, of course, the present, will leave no letters behind it. And in making my reply there is only one question that I can answer or attempt to answer in public; about poetry and its death.

But before I begin, I must own up to those defects, both natural and acquired, which, as you will find, distort and invalidate all that I have to say about poetry. The lack of a sound university training has always made it impossible for me to distinguish between an iambic and a dactyl, and if this were not enough to condemn one for ever, the practice of prose has bred in me, as in most prose writers, a foolish jealousy, a righteous indignation — anyhow, an emotion which the critic should be without. For how, we despised prose writers ask when we get together, could one say what one meant and observe the rules of poetry? Conceive dragging in "blade" because one had mentioned "maid"; and pairing "sorrow" with "borrow"? Rhyme is not only childish, but dishonest, we prose writers say. Then we go on to say, And look at their rules! How easy to be a poet! How strait the path is for them, and how strict! This you must do; this you must not. I would rather be a child and walk in a crocodile down a suburban path than write poetry, I have heard prose writers say. It must be like taking the veil and entering a religious order — observing the rites and rigours of metre. That explains why they repeat the same thing over and over again. Whereas we prose writers (I am only telling you the sort of nonsense prose writers talk when they are alone) are masters of language, not its slaves; nobody can teach us; nobody can coerce us; we say what we mean; we have the whole of life for our province. We are the creators, we are the explorers. . . . So we run on — nonsensically enough, I must admit.

Now that I have made a clean breast of these deficiencies, let us proceed. From certain phrases in your letter I gather that you think that poetry is in a parlous way, and that your case as a poet in this particular autumn Of 1931 is a great deal harder than Shakespeare's, Dryden's, Pope's, or Tennyson's. In fact it is the hardest case that has ever been known. Here you give me an opening, which I am prompt to seize, for a little lecture. Never think yourself singular, never think your own case much harder than other people's. I admit that the age we live in makes this difficult. For the first time in history there are readers — a large body of people, occupied in business, in sport, in nursing their grandfathers, in tying up parcels behind counters — they all read now; and they want to be told how to read and what to read; and their teachers — the reviewers, the lecturers, the broadcasters — must in all humanity make reading easy for them; assure them that literature is violent and exciting, full of heroes and villains; of hostile forces perpetually in conflict; of fields strewn with bones; of solitary victors riding off on white horses wrapped in black cloaks to meet their death at the turn of the road. A pistol shot rings out. "The age of romance was over. The age of realism had begun"— you know the sort of thing. Now of course writers themselves know very well that there is not a word of truth in all this — there are no battles, and no murders and no defeats and no victories. But as it is of the utmost importance that readers should be amused, writers acquiesce. They dress themselves up. They act their parts. One leads; the other follows. One is romantic, the other realist. One is advanced, the other out of date. There is no harm in it, so long as you take it as a joke, but once you believe in it, once you begin to take yourself seriously as a leader or as a follower, as a modern or as a conservative, then you become a self-conscious, biting, and scratching little animal whose work is not of the slightest value or importance to anybody. Think of yourself rather as something much humbler and less spectacular, but to my mind, far more interesting — a poet in whom live all the poets of the past, from whom all poets in time to come will spring. You have a touch of Chaucer in you, and something of Shakespeare; Dryden, Pope, Tennyson — to mention only the respectable among your ancestors — stir in your blood and sometimes move your pen a little to the right or to the left. In short you are an immensely ancient, complex, and continuous character, for which reason please treat yourself with respect and think twice before you dress up as Guy Fawkes and spring out upon timid old ladies at street corners, threatening death and demanding twopence-halfpenny.

However, as you say that you are in a fix ("it has never been so hard to write poetry as it is to-day and that poetry may be, you think, at its last gasp in England the novelists are doing all the interesting things now"), let me while away the time before the post goes in imagining your state and in hazarding one or two guesses which, since this is a letter, need not be taken too seriously or pressed too far. Let me try to put myself in your place; let me try to imagine, with your letter to help me, what it feels like to be a young poet in the autumn of 1931. (And taking my own advice, I shall treat you not as one poet in particular, but as several poets in one.) On the floor of your mind, then — is it not this that makes you a poet? — rhythm keeps up its perpetual beat.

Sometimes it seems to die down to nothing; it lets you eat, sleep, talk like other people. Then again it swells and rises and attempts to sweep all the contents of your mind into one dominant dance. To-night is such an occasion. Although you are alone, and have taken one boot off and are about to undo the other, you cannot go on with the process of undressing, but must instantly write at the bidding of the dance. You snatch pen and paper; you hardly trouble to hold the one or to straighten the other. And while you write, while the first stanzas of the dance are being fastened down, I will withdraw a little and look out of the window. A woman passes, then a man; a car glides to a stop and then — but there is no need to say what I see out of the window, nor indeed is there time, for I am suddenly recalled from my observations by a cry of rage or despair. Your page is crumpled in a ball; your pen sticks upright by the nib in the carpet. If there were a cat to swing or a wife to murder now would be the time. So at least I infer from the ferocity of your expression. You are rasped, jarred, thoroughly out of temper. And if I am to guess the reason, it is, I should say, that the rhythm which was opening and shutting with a force that sent shocks of excitement from your head to your heels has encountered some hard and hostile object upon which it has smashed itself to pieces. Something has worked in which cannot be made into poetry; some foreign body, angular, sharp-edged, gritty, has refused to join in the dance. Obviously, suspicion attaches to Mrs. Gape; she has asked you to make a poem of her; then to Miss Curtis and her confidences on the omnibus; then to C., who has infected you with a wish to tell his story — and a very amusing one it was — in verse. But for some reason you cannot do their bidding. Chaucer could; Shakespeare could; so could Crabbe, Byron, and perhaps Robert Browning. But it is October 1931, and for a long time now poetry has shirked contact with — what shall we call it? — Shall we shortly and no doubt inaccurately call it life? And will you come to my help by guessing what I mean? Well then, it has left all that to the novelist. Here you see how easy it would be for me to write two or three volumes in honour of prose and in mockery of verse; to say how wide and ample is the domain of the one, how starved and stunted the little grove of the other. But it would be simpler and perhaps fairer to check these theories by opening one of the thin books of modern verse that lie on your table. I open and I find myself instantly confused. Here are the common objects of daily prose — the bicycle and the omnibus. Obviously the poet is making his muse face facts. Listen:

Which of you waking early and watching daybreak
Will not hasten in heart, handsome, aware of wonder
At light unleashed, advancing; a leader of movement,
Breaking like surf on turf on road and roof,
Or chasing shadow on downs like whippet racing,
The stilled stone, halting at eyelash barrier,
Enforcing in face a profile, marks of misuse,
Beating impatient and importunate on boudoir shutters
Where the old life is not up yet, with rays
Exploring through rotting floor a dismantled mill —

The old life never to be born again?

Yes, but how will he get through with it? I read on and find:

Whistling as he shuts

His door behind him, travelling to work by tube

Or walking to the park to it to ease the bowels,

and read on and find again

As a boy lately come up from country to town

Returns for the day to his village in EXPENSIVE SHOES—

and so on again to:

Seeking a heaven on earth he chases his shadow,

Loses his capital and his nerve in pursuing

What yachtsmen, explorers, climbers and BUGGERS ARE AFTER.

These lines and the words I have emphasized are enough to confirm me in part of my guess at least. The poet is trying to include Mrs. Gape. He is honestly of opinion that she can be brought into poetry and will do very well there. Poetry, he feels, will be improved by the actual, the colloquial. But though I honour him for the attempt, I doubt that it is wholly successful. I feel a jar. I feel a shock. I feel as if I had stubbed my toe on the corner of the wardrobe. Am I then, I go on to ask, shocked, prudishly and conventionally, by the words themselves? I think not. The shock is literally a shock. The poet as I guess has strained himself to include an emotion that is not domesticated and acclimatized to poetry; the effort has thrown him off his balance; he rights himself, as I am sure I shall find if I turn the page, by a violent recourse to the poetical — he invokes the moon or the nightingale. Anyhow, the transition is sharp. The poem is cracked in the middle. Look, it comes apart in my hands: here is reality on one side, here is beauty on the other; and instead of acquiring a whole object rounded and entire, I am left with broken parts in my hands which, since my reason has been roused and my imagination has not been allowed to take entire possession of me, I contemplate coldly, critically, and with distaste.

Such at least is the hasty analysis I make of my own sensations as a reader; but again I am interrupted. I see that you have overcome your difficulty, whatever it was; the pen is once more in action, and having torn up the first poem you are at work upon another. Now then if I want to understand your state of mind I must invent another explanation to account for this return of fluency. You have dismissed, as I suppose, all sorts of things that would come naturally to your pen if you had been writing prose — the charwoman, the omnibus, the incident on the Channel boat. Your range is restricted — I judge from your expression — concentrated and intensified. I hazard a guess that you are thinking now, not about things in general, but about yourself in particular. There is a fixity, a gloom, yet an inner glow that seem to hint that you are looking within and not without. But in order to consolidate these flimsy guesses about the meaning of an expression on a face, let me open another of the books on your table and check it by what I find there. Again I open at random and read this:

To penetrate that room is my desire,
The extreme attic of the mind, that lies
Just beyond the last bend in the corridor.
Writing I do it. Phrases, poems are keys.
Loving's another way (but not so sure).
A fire's in there, I think, there's truth at last
Deep in a lumber chest. Sometimes I'm near,
But draughts puff out the matches, and I'm lost.
Sometimes I'm lucky, find a key to turn,
Open an inch or two — but always then
A bell rings, someone calls, or cries of "fire"
Arrest my hand when nothing's known or seen,
And running down the stairs again I mourn.
and then this:
There is a dark room,
The locked and shuttered womb,
Where negative's made positive.
Another dark room,
The blind and bolted tomb,
Where positives change to negative.
We may not undo that or escape this, who
Have birth and death coiled in our bones,
Nothing we can do
Will sweeten the real rue,
That we begin, and end, with groans.
And then this:
Never being, but always at the edge of Being
My head, like Death mask, is brought into the Sun.

The shadow pointing finger across cheek,
I move lips for tasting, I move hands for touching,
But never am nearer than touching,
Though the spirit leans outward for seeing.
Observing rose, gold, eyes, an admired landscape,
My senses record the act of wishing
Wishing to be
Rose, gold, landscape or another —
Claiming fulfilment in the act of loving.

Since these quotations are chosen at random and I have yet found three different poets writing about nothing, if not about the poet himself, I hold that the chances are that you too are engaged in the same occupation. I conclude that self offers no impediment; self joins in the dance; self lends itself to the rhythm; it is apparently easier to write a poem about oneself than about any other subject. But what does one mean by "oneself"? Not the self that Wordsworth, Keats, and Shelley have described — not the self that loves a woman, or that hates a tyrant, or that broods over the mystery of the world. No, the self that you are engaged in describing is shut out from all that. It is a self that sits alone in the room at night with the blinds drawn. In other words the poet is much less interested in what we have in common than in what he has apart. Hence I suppose the extreme difficulty of these poems — and I have to confess that it would floor me completely to say from one reading or even from two or three what these poems mean. The poet is trying honestly and exactly to describe a world that has perhaps no existence except for one particular person at one particular moment. And the more sincere he is in keeping to the precise outline of the roses and cabbages of his private universe, the more he puzzles us who have agreed in a lazy spirit of compromise to see roses and cabbages as they are seen, more or less, by the twenty-six passengers on the outside of an omnibus. He strains to describe; we strain to see; he flickers his torch; we catch a flying gleam. It is exciting; it is stimulating; but is that a tree, we ask, or is it perhaps an old woman tying up her shoe in the gutter?

Well, then, if there is any truth in what I am saying — if that is you cannot write about the actual, the colloquial, Mrs. Gape or the Channel boat or Miss Curtis on the omnibus, without straining the machine of poetry, if, therefore, you are driven to contemplate landscapes and emotions within and must render visible to the world at large what you alone can see, then indeed yours is a hard case, and poetry, though still breathing — witness these little books — is drawing her breath in short, sharp gasps. Still, consider the symptoms. They are not the symptoms of death in the least. Death in literature, and I need not tell you how often literature has died in this country or in that, comes gracefully, smoothly, quietly. Lines slip easily down the accustomed grooves. The old designs are copied so glibly that we are half inclined to think them original, save for that very glibness. But here the very opposite is happening: here in my first quotation the poet breaks his machine because he will clog it with raw fact. In my second, he is unintelligible because of his desperate determination to tell the truth about himself. Thus I cannot help thinking that though you may be right in talking of the difficulty of the time, you are wrong to despair.

Is there not, alas, good reason to hope? I say "alas" because then I must give my reasons, which are bound to be foolish and certain also to cause pain to the large and highly respectable society of necrophils — Mr. Peabody, and his like — who much prefer death to life and are even now intoning the sacred and comfortable words, Keats is dead, Shelley is dead, Byron is dead. But it is late: necrophily induces slumber; the old gentlemen have fallen asleep over their classics, and if what I am about to say takes a sanguine tone — and for my part I do not believe in poets dying; Keats, Shelley, Byron are alive here in this room in you and you and you — I can take comfort from the thought that my hoping will not disturb their snoring. So to continue — why should not poetry, now that it has so honestly scraped itself free from certain falsities, the wreckage of the great Victorian age, now that it has so sincerely gone down into the mind of the poet and verified its outlines — a work of renovation that has to be done from time to time and was certainly needed, for bad poetry is almost always the result of forgetting oneself — all becomes distorted and impure if you lose sight of that central reality — now, I say, that poetry has done all this, why should it not once more open its eyes, look out of the window and write about other people? Two or three hundred years ago you were always writing about other people. Your pages were crammed with characters of the most opposite and various kinds — Hamlet, Cleopatra, Falstaff. Not only did we go to you for drama, and for the subtleties of human character, but we also went to you, incredible though this now seems, for laughter. You made us roar with laughter. Then later, not more than a hundred years ago, you were lashing our follies, trouncing our hypocrisies, and dashing off the most brilliant of satires. You were Byron, remember; you wrote Don Juan. You were Crabbe also; you took the most sordid details of the lives of peasants for your theme. Clearly therefore you have it in you to deal with a vast variety of subjects; it is only a temporary necessity that has shut you up in one room, alone, by yourself.

But how are you going to get out, into the world of other people? That is your problem now, if I may hazard a guess — to find the right relationship, now that you know yourself, between the self that you know and the world outside. It is a difficult problem. No living poet has, I think, altogether solved it. And there are a thousand voices prophesying despair. Science, they say, has made poetry impossible; there is no poetry in motor cars and wireless. And we have no religion. All is tumultuous and transitional. Therefore, so people say, there can be no relation between the poet and the present age. But surely that is nonsense. These accidents are superficial; they do not go nearly deep enough to destroy the most profound and primitive of instincts, the instinct of rhythm. All you need now is to stand at the window and let your rhythmical sense open and shut, open and shut, boldly and freely, until one thing melts in another, until the taxis are dancing with the daffodils, until a whole has been made from all these separate fragments. I am talking nonsense, I know. What I mean is, summon all your courage, exert all your vigilance, invoke all the gifts that Nature has been induced to bestow. Then let your rhythmical sense wind itself in and out among men and women, omnibuses, sparrows — whatever come along the street — until it has strung them together in one harmonious whole. That perhaps is your task — to find the relation between things that seem incompatible yet have a mysterious affinity, to absorb every experience that comes your way fearlessly and saturate it completely so that your poem is a whole, not a fragment; to re-think human life into poetry and so give us tragedy again and comedy by means of characters not spun out at length in the novelist's way, but condensed and synthesised in the poet's way-that is what we look to you to do now. But as I do not know what I mean by rhythm nor what I mean by life, and as most certainly I cannot tell you which objects can properly be combined together in a poem — that is entirely your affair — and as I cannot tell a dactyl from an iambic, and am therefore unable to say how you must modify and expand the rites and ceremonies of your ancient and mysterious art — I will move on to safer ground and turn again to these little books themselves.

When, then, I return to them I am, as I have admitted, filled, not with forebodings of death, but with hopes for the future. But one does not always want to be thinking of the future, if, as sometimes happens, one is living in the present.

When I read these poems, now, at the present moment, I find myself — reading, you know, is rather like opening the door to a horde of rebels who swarm out attacking one in twenty places at once — hit, roused, scraped, bared, swung through the air, so that life seems to flash by; then again blinded, knocked on the head — all of which are agreeable sensations for a reader (since nothing is more dismal than to open the door and get no response), and all I believe certain proof that this poet is alive and kicking. And yet mingling with these cries of delight, of jubilation, I record also, as I read, the repetition in the bass of one word intoned over and over again by some malcontent. At last then, silencing the others, I say to this malcontent, "Well, and what do YOU want?" Whereupon he bursts out, rather to my discomfort, "Beauty." Let me repeat, I take no responsibility for what my senses say when I read; I merely record the fact that there is a malcontent in me who complains that it seems to him odd, considering that English is a mixed language, a rich language; a language unmatched for its sound and colour, for its power of imagery and suggestion — it seems to him odd that these modern poets should write as if they had neither ears nor eyes, neither soles to their feet nor palms to their hands, but only honest enterprising book-fed brains, unisexual bodies and — but here I interrupted him. For when it comes to saying that a poet should be bisexual, and that I think is what he was about to say, even I, who have had no scientific training whatsoever, draw the line and tell that voice to be silent.

But how far, if we discount these obvious absurdities, do you think there is truth in this complaint? For my own part now that I have stopped reading, and can see the poems more or less as a whole, I think it is true that the eye and ear are starved of their rights. There is no sense of riches held in reserve behind the admirable exactitude of the lines I have quoted, as there is, for example, behind the exactitude of Mr. Yeats. The poet clings to his one word, his only word, as a drowning man to a spar. And if this is so, I am ready to hazard a reason for it all the more readily because I think it bears out what I have just been saying. The art of writing, and that is perhaps what my malcontent means by "beauty," the art of having at one's beck and call every word in the language, of knowing their weights, colours, sounds, associations, and thus making them, as is so necessary in English, suggest more than they can state, can be learnt of course to some extent by reading — it is impossible to read too much; but much more drastically and effectively by imagining that one is not oneself but somebody different. How can you learn to write if you write only about one single person? To take the obvious example. Can you doubt that the reason why Shakespeare knew every sound and syllable in the language and could do precisely what he liked with grammar and syntax, was that Hamlet, Falstaff and Cleopatra rushed him into this knowledge; that the lords, officers, dependants, murderers and common soldiers of the plays insisted that he should say exactly what they felt in the words expressing their feelings? It was they who taught him to write, not the begetter of the

Sonnets. So that if you want to satisfy all those senses that rise in a swarm whenever we drop a poem among them — the reason, the imagination, the eyes, the ears, the palms of the hands and the soles of the feet, not to mention a million more that the psychologists have yet to name, you will do well to embark upon a long poem in which people as unlike yourself as possible talk at the tops of their voices. And for heaven's sake, publish nothing before you are thirty.

That, I am sure, is of very great importance. Most of the faults in the poems I have been reading can be explained, I think, by the fact that they have been exposed to the fierce light of publicity while they were still too young to stand the strain. It has shrivelled them into a skeleton austerity, both emotional and verbal, which should not be characteristic of youth. The poet writes very well; he writes for the eye of a severe and intelligent public; but how much better he would have written if for ten years he had written for no eye but his own! After all, the years from twenty to thirty are years (let me refer to your letter again) of emotional excitement. The rain dripping, a wing flashing, someone passing — the commonest sounds and sights have power to fling one, as I seem to remember, from the heights of rapture to the depths of despair. And if the actual life is thus extreme, the visionary life should be free to follow. Write then, now that you are young, nonsense by the ream. Be silly, be sentimental, imitate Shelley, imitate Samuel Smiles; give the rein to every impulse; commit every fault of style, grammar, taste, and syntax; pour out; tumble over; loose anger, love, satire, in whatever words you can catch, coerce or create, in whatever metre, prose, poetry, or gibberish that comes to hand. Thus you will learn to write. But if you publish, your freedom will be checked; you will be thinking what people will say; you will write for others when you ought only to be writing for yourself. And what point can there be in curbing the wild torrent of spontaneous nonsense which is now, for a few years only, your divine gift in order to publish prim little books of experimental verses? To make money? That, we both know, is out of the question. To get criticism? But you friends will pepper your manuscripts with far more serious and searching criticism than any you will get from the reviewers. As for fame, look I implore you at famous people; see how the waters of dullness spread around them as they enter; observe their pomposity, their prophetic airs; reflect that the greatest poets were anonymous; think how Shakespeare cared nothing for fame; how Donne tossed his poems into the waste-paper basket; write an essay giving a single instance of any modern English writer who has survived the disciples and the admirers, the autograph hunters and the interviewers, the dinners and the luncheons, the celebrations and the commemorations with which English society so effectively stops the mouths of its singers and silences their songs.

But enough. I, at any rate, refuse to be necrophilus. So long as you and you and you, venerable and ancient representatives of Sappho, Shakespeare, and Shelley are aged precisely twenty-three and propose — 0 enviable lot! — to spend the next fifty years of your lives in writing poetry, I refuse to think that the art is dead. And if ever the temptation to necrophilize comes over you, be warned by the fate of that old gentleman whose name I forget, but I think that it was Peabody. In the very act of consigning all the arts to the grave he choked over a large piece of hot buttered toast and the consolation then offered him that he was about to join the elder Pliny in the shades gave him, I am told, no sort of satisfaction whatsoever.

And now for the intimate, the indiscreet, and indeed, the only really interesting parts of this letter. . . .

CPSIA information can be obtained
at www.ICGtesting.com
Printed in the USA
BVHW07s1026240718
522489BV00001BA/108/P